Dear Parent:
Your child's love of reading starts here!

Every child learns to read in a different way and at his or her own speed. Some go back and forth between reading levels and read favorite books again and again. Others read through each level in order. You can help your young reader improve and become more confident by encouraging his or her own interests and abilities. From books your child reads with you to the first books he or she reads alone, there are I Can Read Books for every stage of reading:

SHARED READING
Basic language, word repetition, and whimsical illustrations, ideal for sharing with your emergent reader

BEGINNING READING
Short sentences, familiar words, and simple concepts for children eager to read on their own

READING WITH HELP
Engaging stories, longer sentences, and language play for developing readers

READING ALONE
Complex plots, challenging vocabulary, and high-interest topics for the independent reader

ADVANCED READING
Short paragraphs, chapters, and exciting themes for the perfect bridge to chapter books

I Can Read Books have introduced children to the joy of reading since 1957. Featuring award-winning authors and illustrators and a fabulous cast of beloved characters, I Can Read Books set the standard for beginning readers.

A lifetime of discovery begins with the magical words "I Can Read!"

Visit www.icanread.com for information
on enriching your child's reading experience.

Pinkalicious®
Pinkie Promise

For Marjorie and Bob,
thank you for your support and guidance.
—V.K.

The author gratefully acknowledges
the artistic and editorial contributions
of Daniel Griffo and Susan Hill.

I Can Read Book® is a trademark of HarperCollins Publishers.

Pinkalicious: Pinkie Promise
Copyright © 2011 by Victoria Kann

PINKALICIOUS and all related logos and characters
are trademarks of Victoria Kann. Used with permission.

Based on the HarperCollins book *Pinkalicious* written by
Victoria Kann and Elizabeth Kann, illustrated by Victoria Kann

Library of Congress catalog card number: 2010941914
ISBN 978-0-06-192888-8 (trade bdg.) —ISBN 978-0-06-192887-1 (pbk.)

14 15 16 SCP 10 9 8 7
❖
First Edition

I Can Read!

BEGINNING READING 1

Pinkalicious®
Pinkie Promise

by Victoria Kann

HARPER
An Imprint of HarperCollinsPublishers

I was making a picture
for my teacher, Mr. Pushkin.
I ran out of my favorite color.

I asked my friend Alison

if I could borrow her paints.

"Just don't use up all the pink," she said.

"I won't," I said.

"I promise."

I worked very hard on the picture.

It looked good.

I gave the picture to Mr. Pushkin.

"What a terrific painting!" he said.

"It's so pink."

"You mean it's pinkerrific!" I said.

Alison was coming over
to get her paint set.

Some of the colors were empty.

Uh-oh.

What was I going to do?

"Um . . . I'm sorry, Alison," I said.

"By mistake I used up all the pink."

Alison frowned.

"You also used up all the red

and the white," she said.

"Well, red and white make pink,

so really it's all pink," I said.

Alison was angry.

"You said you wouldn't use up
all the pink paint!" said Alison.
"You promised."
"I'm really really sorry, Alison,"
I said again.
Alison took her paint set
and walked away.

Alison did not sit with me at lunch.

I sat alone.

I ate my jelly sandwich.

Jelly does not taste pink-a-yummy

if you are eating all by yourself.

Then I thought of something.

I went back to the classroom.

I made Alison a card to apologize.

"This card is very blue,"

I said to Alison.

"There were no other colors.

Almost everybody is out of pink."

21

"Thanks for the card," Alison said.

"It's not just beautiful, it's bluetiful."

"Alison," I asked,

"can we still be friends?"

"Of course we're friends,
Pinkalicious," Alison said.
"I'm sorry I got angry
about the paint.
I won't get so mad next time."

I was so happy!

"Let's play this weekend!" I said.

When Alison came over to play,

I had a surprise for her.

I gave Alison a new tube of paint.

"It's not even my birthday!"

said Alison.

"And that's not all," I said.

"Guess what?"

We got ice cream!

We shared a pink peppermint ice cream sundae with raspberry swirl syrup.

The sundae had two cherries on top
so we could each have our own.
Some things are just too hard to share!

PLEASING POMEGRANATE PUNCH

MAGENTA MINT MANGO

PINK PEPPERMINT

PLUM PINK PERFECTION

"Let's always be friends,"
Alison said.
"Yes, that would be funtastic,"
I said.

"Let's make it a pinkie promise!"
we said at the same time.
"Pinkie promises last forever,"
I said happily.